Little Big Cat
Gato Pequeño y Grande

Learn to Read Series
Book 16

Cataloging-in-Publication Data

Sargent, Dave, 1941–
    Little Big Cat = Gato Pequeño y Grande /
by Dave and Pat Sargent ; illustrated by
Laura Robinson.—Prairie Grove, AR :
Ozark Publishing, c2004.
        p. cm. (Learn to read series ; 16)

    Bilingual.
    Cover title.
    SUMMARY: A little cat is a fast cat!
He chases dogs and eats dog tails!
    ISBN 1-56763-991-7 (hc)
            1-56763-992-5 (pbk)

    [1. Animals—Fiction.] I. Sargent, Pat, 1936–
II. Robinson, Laura, 1973– ill. III. Title.
IV. Series.
    PZ7.S2465Ic 2004
    [E]—dc21   00-012635

Printed in the United States of America

Little Big Cat
Gato Pequeño y Grande

Learn to Read Series
Book 16

By Dave and Pat Sargent

Illustrated by Laura Robinson

Ozark Publishing, Inc.
P.O. Box 228
Prairie Grove, AR 72753

Dave and Pat Sargent, authors of the extremely popular Animal Pride Series, plus many other Accelerated Reader books, visit schools all over the United States, free of charge.

If you would like to have Dave and Pat visit your school, please ask your librarian to call 1-800-321-5671.

Little Big Cat
Gato Pequeño y Grande

Learn to Read Series
Book 16

I am Little Big Cat. That is my name.

Soy Gato Pequeño y Grande. Ese es mi nombre.

I can run very fast. I am a fast cat!

Yo puedo correr muy rápido. Yo soy un gato veloz.

I love to play. I love to play ball.

Me gusta jugar. Me gusta jugar a la pelota.

I play ball with Mamma. I play ball with Daddy.

Yo juego a la pelota con Mamá. Yo juego a la pelota con Papá.

I chase dogs. I chase big dogs.

Yo cazo perros. Yo cazo perros grandes.

I eat dog tails. I eat big dog tails.

Me como las colas de perros. Me como las colas de perros grandes.

I eat mice. I love to eat mice.

Me como ratones. Me gusta comer ratones.

I eat big mice. I love to eat big mice.

Me como ratones grandes. Me gusta comer ratones grandes.

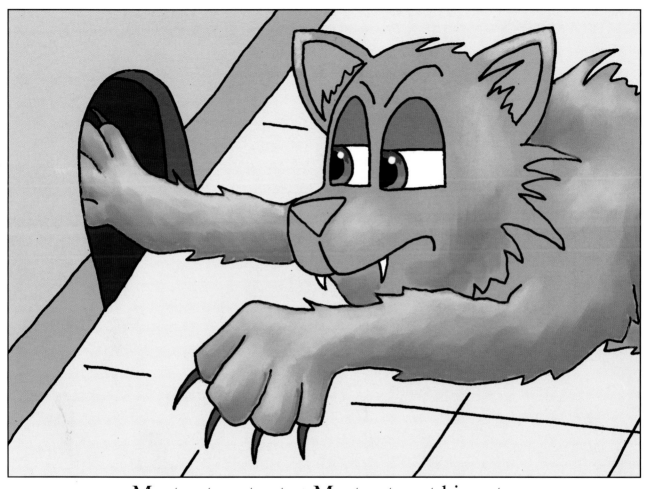

Most cats eat rats. Most cats eat big rats.

Casi todo los gatos comen ratas.
Casi todo los gatos comen ratas grandes.

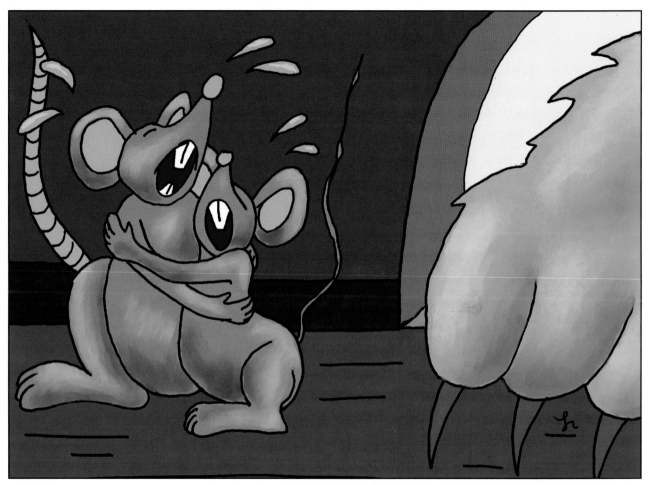

I eat rats. I eat big rats.

Me como ratas. Me como ratas grandes.

I eat bones. I eat big bones.

Me como huesos. Me como huesos grandes.

When the dog is not here, I take his bones.

Cuando el perro no está aquí, me robo sus huesos.

Most cats are lazy. Most cats sleep late.

Casi todos los gatos son perezosos.
Casi todos los gatos duermen tarde.

I am lazy. I sleep late.

Yo soy perezoso. Yo duermo tarde.

I have long claws. My claws are strong.

Yo tengo garras largas. Mis garras son fuertes.

I scratch dogs. I scratch big dogs.

Yo araño perros. Yo araño perros grandes.

I climb trees. I climb big trees.

Yo trepo los árboles. Yo trepo los árboles grandes.

I may be little but I am big. I am Little Big Cat.

Pueda ser que soy pequeño pero soy grande.
Soy Gato Pequeño y Grande.